SERVANTS OF THE GREAT ONE

The Chronicles of Dusty

SERVANTS OF THE GREAT ONE

MICHAEL ANTHONY KELLY

TATE PUBLISHING
AND **ENTERPRISES**, LLC

Published by Tate Publishing & Enterprises, LLC
127 E. Trade Center Terrace | Mustang, Oklahoma 73064 USA
1.888.361.9473 | www.tatepublishing.com

Tate Publishing is committed to excellence in the publishing industry. The company reflects the philosophy established by the founders, based on Psalm 68:11,
"The Lord gave the word and great was the company of those who published it."

Book design copyright © 2014 by Tate Publishing, LLC. All rights reserved.
Cover design by Joel Uber
Interior design by Jomar Ouano

Published in the United States of America

ISBN: 978-1-62902-931-3
Fiction / General
13.12.03

DEDICATION

To my little boy, Thomas Wyatt Kelly, whose wonderful imagination inspired my own.

CONTENTS

DUSTY

The day began as most days. Dusty is an orange Maine Coon cat that lives at Three Rivers Apartment Complex in Columbia, South Carolina. It was a beautiful overcast evening, and there was a cool breeze fluttering through Dusty's fur as he sat on the balcony on the second floor of his master's duplex.

Dusty was quietly enjoying the silence of the evening, only disturbed by the rustling of the leaves. Then suddenly, his quiet rest was disturbed.

"If dad servant sees you sitting out there, you are history, you oaf!"

Dusty cringed at the voice of his arch antagonist. There, sitting at the base of the sliding glass door was Priscilla. Priscilla was the beautiful Himalayan Persian that lived in the house with Dusty. It was rumored that she was descended from royalty, but only she knew for sure.

"What is it, Priscilla?" asked Dusty. "I was just beginning to believe there could be a world without pain. Then you showed up."

"Quiet, you uncultured oaf!" retorted Priscilla. "Just wait until mom and dad servant return. I shall convey my displeasure with your attitude."

How ridiculous, thought Dusty. *Every educated cat knows that humans cannot comprehend the complex nature of the language of Catdomnese.*

But nonetheless, Priscilla would try every night to convey her complaints to mom and dad servant, but to no avail. All mom servant would do would be to go to the cabinet and give her another snack. This did nothing for Priscilla's disposition, though her expanse increased each time.

Priscilla, feeling quite sure she made her point, continued with the conversation, "Though I don't know why the Great Cat Council has requested your presence tonight."

"Me?" retorted Dusty. "Whatever for?"

"I just said I had no idea, you oaf!" snapped Priscilla. "Just be ready in an hour so we can make preparations for getting underway."

Dusty sat there on the balcony, overwhelmed by the news Priscilla had just presented to him. *Why would they want to talk with me?* thought Dusty.

The Great Cat Council was formed centuries ago once it was determined that the path to survival laid with the breed of animals called humans. Though humans seem to have very limited avenues of communication, they make great strives in building shelters and growing food, and they seem to place great value on short, green-looking paper. This seems a great mystery in the vast cat kingdom, but the cat race just accepts these truths without question. For when humans give each other these small strips of green paper, the cats benefit by receiving meals in small metal containers and in pouches of various sizes made also from paper.

All of those facts aside, Dusty still had no answer for this new invitation from the Great Cat Council. Since the time of the great Serval cat kingdom in Egypt, the council only allowed purebred cats to sit on the council. The only explanation for this prejudice is that during the time of the serval kingdom, the tabby and calico cats had not fully come to be. The tabby and calico breeds were not considered pure, and thus over time, they were shunned by the pure breeds. These were the facts, and Dusty knew them. So why did the council want to throw tradition into the litter box and allow a common cat to enter? Dusty was, by all accounts, a Maine Coon, but that was not an established fact. Dusty's mom was a homeless Maine Coon in Savannah, Georgia, when she gave birth to Dusty. But Dusty's father and his breed were never known or recorded with the Maine Coon council of the chapter of Georgia. Thus, Dusty was a commoner and, by virtue of that fact, shunned.

THE GREAT CAT COUNCIL

Priscilla came back an hour later with a beautiful black cat in tow. It was Saja, the newest member at the complex. Saja was a domestic black cat that wanted to win friends in high places. Somehow, Priscilla convinced Saja that it would increase his chances if he would take the job of being her butler. Dusty knew that Priscilla would never introduce Saja to the upper crust, but he thought, *Oh let him figure it out for himself.*

"Are you quite ready to leave, you uncultured oaf?" retorted Priscilla.

"Quite ready!" snapped Dusty. "I have been waiting for a chance to tell those high-nose, snooty felines what I think about their unjustified prejudice."

"You will say nothing to ruin my social standing," replied Priscilla, breathless from Dusty's threat.

"Please, madam. Remember your blood pressure." said Saja, holding Priscilla's paw.

"Yes, you're quite right, Saja."

"Good grief, Saja!" yelled Dusty. "You're the biggest paw kisser I have ever seen. Where is your self respect?"

"Enough!" shouted Priscilla. "We must get going. The council meets in half an hour, and we still have to sneak past mom and dad servant before we get there."

Luck was with the little crew as they crept past mom and dad servant asleep on the sofa as the television played the national anthem softly. All three cats walked quietly out the pet door, off the front stoop, and down the small street the apartment complex was on.

After about fifteen minutes of walking, the little crew turned right onto Greystone Boulevard and started toward the "Riverbanks Zoo. The night was beautiful and soft, and the street was full of cats of every shape and size, all heading toward the zoo.

As Dusty walked along with Priscilla, he noticed many of the cats walking along with them were tabbies and calicos.

"Priscilla, it pains me to ask you a question, but curiosity will allow me no other option," said Dusty. "If the non-pure breeds are not socially acceptable to you purebloods, then why are so many going to this meeting?"

"Necessity, you oaf!" snapped Priscilla. "In order to keep the peasant class from revolting, we allow them to come to all of the meetings. But it is understood that they have no vote in political issues."

"So I am not allowed to vote in political matters, but I am okay to do the litter box work, eh?" retorted Dusty.

Priscilla gave Dusty a stern but understanding glance. It was not long before the crowd of cats made it across the overpass on Greystone Boulevard, passing the great building the humans called the South Carolina Baptist Convention.

Saja felt horribly small next to the building as they walked by.

"What do the humans do there?" wondered Saja.

"It is rumored that they worship the Great Lion as we do. But I find that hard to believe with their inability to speak in any known feline tongue," said Priscilla smugly.

Dusty bit his tongue to keep from gasping as the tall, dark walls of the Riverbanks Zoo came into view. The long, assorted procession filed its way through the small secret entrance in the natural vegetation by the main zoo gate. Standing there by the entrance was a spider monkey checking off the names and breeds of each cat as they filed by.

"Name, please?" asked the spider monkey.

Priscilla approached. "Why, yes," replied Priscilla. "I am Countess Priscilla of the house of the Kelly servants, and this is my butler, Saja." Priscilla pointed to Saja. "He is of the servant line from the country of Korea."

Priscilla said this because dad servant acquired Saja while traveling with the human pride called US Army. It was customary to give the last name of the servants that took care of you, and in this case, the little group of three lived in the Kelly home.

"Enter!" replied the spider monkey.

Dusty stepped up after Priscilla.

"Breed?" asked the monkey.

"Dusty of the Maine Coons of Savannah."

"Sorry, sir. Your line is not recorded here," said the spider monkey in a very businesslike tone.

Before Dusty could reply, a voice rang out from the darkness.

"It's okay, Sergeant."

Dusty turned toward the direction of the comment. Gradually a beautiful golden-spotted cheetah came into view under the light of the entrance.

"Who are you?" Dusty asked.

"I am Domingo, captain of the guard for King Alfanso. You may enter."

Dusty hesitated for a moment and then continued on his way. There was no point in continuing the conversation since Domingo had already walked away.

Dusty walked through a small dark path into a large opening. He could see the outline of the great carrousel and various buildings. He continued following the procession of cats on the now-smooth brick walkway leading toward the botanical gardens. The procession turned off the main path and stopped at the location of the old bridge ruins in the forest. All purebred cats were sitting closest to the stage on the tallest and yet flattest group of stones in the ruins. The tabby and calico breeds sat at the outer edges. It was here that Dusty took his seat on a comfortable rock that had a good view.

A full moon shined in the clear night sky. The moonlight pierced through a natural opening in the canopy of the treetops, forming a perfect light on the stage. Then from the shadows, Domingo, captain of the guard, rose from the shadows and appeared under the light.

"Hear ye, hear ye!" announced Domingo. "The honorable and distinguished his Royal Highness King Alfanso, ruler of the Carolina realm."

All at once, every cat in the audience bowed as Domingo stepped out of the light, and the great golden lion stepped in his place. The lion wore a beautiful golden coat, and his mane circled around his handsome head.

"Cats of the great clans and breeds," said Alfanso. "Welcome to this special assembly. As you know, we were not scheduled to meet for another month, but circumstances have forced our hand."

"What circumstances would that be, great king?" asked a tall black calico.

"A just question, Semeon, prince of the calicos," said Alfanso. "We have received a letter of urgency from the delegation of the Maine Coon pride. It seems that all of the female royalty of the Maine Coon pride is disappearing. We know this only by the limited *Catdomnese* language in the letter. The Maine Coon princess of the Carolinas is here with us tonight."

Suddenly, another light appeared through the canopy of the trees. There in the new light stood a beautiful white Maine Coon cat.

"*Baguma tori honi, catos Carolinas*," said the white Maine Coon.

"Does anyone possibly know what the princess just said?" asked Alfanso. Low whispers roared throughout the crowd of shocked felines.

"She says, 'Hello to all of the cats of the Carolinas,'" your grace," said a voice at the back of the group.

"Wonderful!" shouted Alfanso. "Who said that? Please come forward and identify yourself."

Cats began to back up and make a natural path as the cat in question moved through the crowd with only a raised tail visible. Then all at once, Dusty appeared at the foot of the stone stage.

"I said it, your grace," said Dusty. "I am Dusty, son of the Maine Coons of Savannah."

"Outstanding!" shouted Alfanso. "Would you do us the honor of translating?"

"I cannot, my lord," replied Dusty.

Gasps rang out from the crowd. Priscilla let out a loud groan and, once again, fainted in the arms of Saja. Alfanso raised his paw to summon the group to be quiet.

"I am afraid I don't understand, sir Dusty," said Alfanso. "Would you please explain?"

"Yes, my lord," replied Dusty. "I am what many of the social elite refer to as a half breed. I cannot even hold a seat in this court. Since that is the case, I am not bound to help this court nor am I inclined to serve a king that does not claim me as one of his own. I have no king, and I have no court to serve."

The crowd went wild with gasps and shouts of "Banish him, banish him." Domingo appeared from the shadows and whispered in Alfanso's ear, "Your grace, the penalty for speaking to the king in this way is death. What are your orders?"

"Silence!" roared Alfanso. "I said silence!"

A desperate quiet fell on the crowd. Alfanso raised his paw to Domingo, dismissing him.

"Your points are well thought out and in order, sir Dusty," said Alfanso. "So tell me what the answer to this riddle might be. We need your help, but you are not a member of this court and, as the law stands now, cannot ever be. So what do you propose, Dusty, son of Maine Coons?"

"Quite simple, my lord," said Dusty. "Equality!"

Once again the crowd gasped.

"Quiet!" roared Alfanso. "Then name your terms, Dusty, son of Savannah Maine Coons."

"Very well, your grace," replied Dusty. "If I translate, all those who are half breeds will be declared a pride. A pride in good standing with the court."

"And?" asked Alfanso.

"And the pride will be given the right to have representation in your court with an equal voice and vote," continued Dusty.

Laughter rang out from the crowd.

"You ask for something that has not occurred for a thousand years." Alfanso chuckled.

"Neither has there been a need for a translator in your court, your grace," replied Dusty. "Desperate times call for exceptions to present laws. Wouldn't you agree, your grace?"

The laughter in the crowd turned silent, and the grin on Alfanso's face waxed to a frown.

"It would appear, sir Dusty, that you hold all of the cards," said Alfanso. "I will agree to half of your demands up front and the rest after you translate, if your translation is to my liking. Before you translate, I will agree to declare the half breeds a formal pride in their own right. The rest will be considered after you translate."

"Considered, not granted?" questioned Dusty.

"Take it, or leave it!" roared Alfanso. "I will search the world over for another translator before I am blackmailed into anything more."

"Time is not a luxury you have, my lord," interrupted Dusty. "Or is it?"

Alfanso thought for a moment and replied, "All right. I will agree to your terms, but with a counter proposal.

"Anything, my lord," shouted Dusty with a wide grin.

"These rights will apply to all half breeds save one. You pick the half breed that will remain an outcast. And remember, these rights only apply to my kingdom. What other kings do in their realm is none of my concern. Only the great king of the African realm can make equality worldwide. I am only a vassal king. Do you agree?"

Dusty, looking down to the ground, replied, "Yes, my lord, I do."

"And who will be the one half breed that will not share in these rights?" asked Alfanso.

"It will be me, my lord," replied Dusty.

"So be it," said Alfanso. "Proceed with the translation."

Dusty stepped up on the stone stage and escorted the beautiful Maine Coon princess to the side of the stage so they could talk in private.

THE QUEST

It had been about an hour since Dusty had escorted the beautiful Maine Coon princess to the side of the stage. The crowd was getting restless, and King Alfanso was conferring nervously with Domingo when the private conference was interrupted.

"I am ready, your grace!" shouted Dusty.

The crowd fell silent.

"You may step forward and report to the delegation."

Dusty walked over to the main spotlight on the floor and stood.

"It seems the Maine Coon pride is in desperate need of our help. Various Maine Coon spies throughout the world have acquired the identity of the one kidnapping the royal female Maine Coons. It's Coal, the prince of panthers."

The crowd went wild with shouts, meows, hisses, and whispers.

"But how can this be?" asked Alfanso. "Coal was stationed at the El Paso Zoo until a month ago, when he died in an accident."

"He faked his death, my lord," replied Dusty.

"But how?" asked Alfanso.

"That's not as important as what he is planning, your grace. He plans to overthrow the kingdom of the African realm."

"What does that have to do with the kidnapping of all the royal females?" shouted Domingo.

"The world is ruled by the humans!" shouted Dusty. "Now even though the cats are served by our pet humans, they provide us with much. Coal plans on making the Maine Coon princesses his wives. His offspring will look like ordinary cats, but they will possess the strength and evil of their father. Once humans start serving this new pride, they will manipulate our humans, and through them, they will rule the world."

"But why the Maine Coons?" asked Domingo.

"Why not any cat pride? For over one hundred years, the Maine Coons have been known as the gentile giants," replied Dusty. "They are desired by humans for their size, beauty, and gentleness with their cubs. If Coal can harness all of that, the humans will be lining up to serve these cats."

"Then we must act now!" shouted Alfanso.

"I will gather a strike force at once, sir," replied Domingo.

"No!" said Alfanso. "Coal must not be underestimated. If he is clever enough to kidnap a band of Maine Coon females, he is clever enough to have an army. If we send a strike force, he will be waiting. A large or small force would be easily detected by his spies."

"Then what shall we do, my lord?" asked Domingo.

"We shall send one cat and one cat only to stop him," said Alfanso.

"Who?" asked Domingo.

"Dismiss the delegation," replied Alfanso. "Bring Sir Dusty and the Maine Coon princess to my chambers."

THE CHAMBERS

A half hour later in the chambers of King Alfanso, Dusty stood beside the Maine Coon princess, waiting for Alfanso to appear. The room was much like any chambers one would find at a zoo. Cement walls, plenty of straw about with a wonderful bed in the corner and a pan full of red juicy steak. Dusty's mouth watered at the succulent meal. The princess began to speak to Dusty in the Maine Coon language.

"Sir Dusty!"

"Yes, my lady," replied Dusty.

"I know of your mother's side of Savannah Maine Coons."

"You do?" asked Dusty. "I have no memory of my mother and have absolutely no knowledge of my father. Please tell me everything."

"Well, I don't know everything." The princess chuckled. "However, I will tell you what I know. I looked up the records of the Savannah pride before I came to this gathering. The scribe of Savannah translated the writings and sent them to me. It seems your mother's name was Custard. She was declared a princess of the Savannah realm called Abercorn. She lived next to some of the marshland there. She was to be wed to one of the Maine Coons of the Candler realm. She fell in love with another. She lost her title, and her true love was lost in a storm of the marshes. Also, she gave birth to you and two others in the hollow of a tree trunk. You were gathered by two human servants and taken into their home. They are the Kellys who you now live with."

"Why did they take me from my mother?" asked Dusty.

"She was ill to the point of death, and her milk had run dry. She brought the Kellys to the tree in hope that they would agree to be your servants," said the princess.

"Then who was my father?" asked Dusty.

"There is only one reason he would not be recorded in the domestic records, my knight," said the princess. "He was wild."

Dusty's mouth fell open. Suddenly, the king appeared with Domingo beside him.

"Stand two guards at the door, captain," ordered Alfanso. "See to it that we are not disturbed."

Domingo bowed his head and left to carry out his duties.

"Sir Dusty, it is quite fortuitous that you could speak Maine Coon," said Alfanso.

"I was told by the older cats, my lord, that there was no such thing as luck," said Dusty. "The elders say the Great One directs all things."

"As I also believe," replied Alfanso. "Now let us get down to business. Dusty! *Toleno atobo noco*?" asked Alfanso.

"No, my lord, I don't care for anything," replied Dusty before he realized what he had done. Dusty understood this odd language, but how?

"My suspicion was correct!" shouted Alfanso with a grin.

"What language did you speak, my lord?"

It is the language of the cats of the wild. Only those cats that have wild blood flowing through their veins can understand its usage," said Alfanso.

Dusty stood silent for a moment.

"Who is my father, my lord?" asked Dusty.

"I looked up your history in our archives here," replied Alfanso. "Your father's name was Juno. He was prince of the Savannah bobcats. He fell in love with your mother, Custard, at a most crucial time in our history. Your father was a guardian of the domestic cats of the Savannah realm. One night, a salt water gator wandered out of the marsh near your mother's home. Juno sacrificed himself for your mother."

"How brave!" said Dusty.

"How unfortunate," said Alfanso. "To fall in love with a cat from the domestic line is forbidden. If the gator had not intervened, the council of wildcats probably would have sent him into exile. Had we known you and your siblings existed, you would have been exiled as well."

"Why, my lord?" asked Dusty.

"We did not know what the result would be," replied Alfanso. "Until now! You possess not only the ability to speak ordinary *Catdomnese* but Maine Coon as well. And now you also can speak the language of the cats of the wild. Beyond that, we shall just have to see."

Alfanso strolled over to his bed and stretched out. He then took one of the beautiful red-looking steaks from the pan and began eating as he talked.

"I assume by this time you have gathered that I am sending you on this quest to save the cat world?" asked Alfanso.

"So I gathered, your grace," replied Dusty. "Why you seem to be sure I will go eludes me though."

"Quite simple, my boy!" replied Alfanso. "In my estimation, you simply have no alternative. Would you care for me to explain?"

"Oh, please do, your grace," replied Dusty with a sarcastic tone.

"You see, my boy, Coal will be looking for an army as we all know. He is wild, so we need someone that is wild. The females are Maine Coon, so we clearly need someone that speaks Maine Coon. Plus our network of spies is made up of mostly domestic cats speaking *Catdomnese* so it pays to be fluent in that as well. Now let me see, out of the whole Carolinas, who can speak all three languages? Hmmmmmm oh why, that would be you! Congratulations, my boy!"

"Wildcats know, *Catdomnese* my lord," shouted Dusty.

"Yes, well, the last time I checked, sir, the zoo gets upset when wildcats roam around Columbia!" retorted Alfanso while eating the last of his steak.

Alfanso licked the steak juice from his paw and walked over to Dusty.

"You came very close, my boy, to making me quite angry. At any rate, let me put it another way, sir. You will do this for me, the Maine Coons, and the world, or there will simply be no cat kingdom for half breeds to take a part in."

Dusty saw the logic of the king's argument.

"Do I make myself clear, sir Dusty?" asked Alfanso.

Dusty bowed his head and in the best sarcastic southern accent he could muster replied, "I do yield, sir, and tremble in the presence of your fiery intellect."

"I'll take that as a yes!" replied Alfanso. "You will leave first thing in the morning. Domingo will brief you for the mission."

"Well, where am I going, my lord?" asked Dusty.

"Where the quest began, my boy," replied Alfanso. "In El Paso."

THE TRAIL OF A WILDCAT

It was morning. Dusty stood up from his soft bed and stretched. Mom servant came walking through the room and took time to stroke his broad back.

"Hi, darling! How's momma's big boy?"

Dusty loved mom servant's love for pets. She continued out of the room and, Dusty, scratching his head, said, "I had the strangest dream last night!"

"It was no dream, you oaf!" proclaimed Priscilla as she entered the room with Saja in tow.

"It wasn't?" exclaimed Dusty. You mean, I really do have a mission to leave on?"

"Unfortunately, yes," replied Priscilla. "Our biggest challenge now will be in how we sneak you out of the house."

"So what's the plan, blueblood?" asked Dusty.

"You tell me!" snapped Priscilla. "We have enough trouble without you making passes at royalty."

Suddenly a blue jay lit on the stoop outside the sliding glass doors where Dusty, Priscilla, and Saja were standing.

"Airmail," shouted the bird.

Priscilla motioned to Saja, and he opened the sliding glass door and received a small piece of paper from the bird.

"It's from Captain Domingo of the Riverbanks Zoo, my lady," said Saja.

"Oh good. Read it, my boy," replied Priscilla.

> Circumstances have changed. Must leave tonight on your mission. Be at the Riverbanks Zoo tonight at 10:00 p.m.
>
> Domingo

"What!" shouted Dusty. "We can't come up with a plan to get past mom and dad servant that quick! If I just leave, then Mom will be worried sick."

"Allow me to worry about that, my champion," came a voice from the closet. Dusty turned around, and the beautiful Maine Coon princess emerged from the bedroom closet.

Dusty gasped. "But how? But where did you—"

"A secret passage, my hero," replied the princess in Maine Coon.

"What are you two talking about?" demanded Priscilla as she bowed toward the Maine Coon princess.

"We were just talking about various ways to expose you for the grouch you are," replied Dusty.

"Quiet, you oaf!" shouted Priscilla, angered that anyone would dare question her temperament.

"Before you came in, Priscilla, the princess was about to reveal a plan for getting me out of here without mom and dad servant getting worried," replied Dusty.

I will need some time-and-coat coloring, but I think my plan will work," said the princess in Maine Coon.

"Very well, princess," replied Dusty.

"By the way, Your Highness, I get the impression that you also speak Catomnese fluently."

The princess smiled sheepishly. "What gave you that impression, my hero?"

"At the council meeting and at our little talk with the king, you just looked like you understood everything that was going on," replied Dusty.

"This is outrageous!" shouted Priscilla. "The entire Cat council was jumping through cat condos to find a translator, and you speak the common cat tongue? You are my kind of royalty." Priscilla bowed in admiration.

"Priscilla, countess of Persians, would you do me the honor of assisting me in my preparation?" asked the princess as she reached down to help Priscilla rise from her homage.

"I would be honored, my lady."

Both the princess and Priscilla walked into the bathroom and closed the door. Two hours later, Priscilla emerged from the bathroom. Dusty and Saja stood from their resting mats.

"May I present the Maine Coon princess, Sir Dusty!" shouted Priscilla as a familiar-looking orange Maine Coon cat emerged from the bathroom. The cat was the absolute twin of Dusty. Dusty moved closer to his twin. Sniffing at the mirror image of himself, he recognized the perfume the cat was wearing.

"Is that really you, Princess?"

"Why yes, my lord. It is I."

"Well, that answers my question on how I am going to get past mom and dad servant," replied Dusty.

"Dusk is upon us, my lord," said the princess. "You must move quickly if you plan to reach the zoo by nightfall."

Dusty quickly moved to the second-story balcony sliding glass doors that had been opened. Dusty jumped to the balcony rail and looked back at the princess.

"I just thought, my lady, what may I call you?" asked Dusty.

"My name is Lydia," she replied. "You may call me Lydia."

Dusty smiled and jumped from the balcony rail to the tree just off the rail. He quickly climbed down and hurried off through the apartment complex as the dusk of the Carolina day slowly turned to darkness.

THE HUNT

Dusty arrived at the entrance of the Riverbanks Zoo as darkness finally took hold of the evening. Domingo rose from behind a nearby palm tree.

"Psst! Psst?"

Dusty turned to see the dimly illuminated Cheetah and then ran over to him.

"You are right on time, Dusty!" said Domingo. "It would appear that time is no longer with us."

"What do you mean?" asked Dusty.

"General David, head of the red-tailed hawks, said his El Paso intelligence network has revealed that one of the Maine Coon females has agreed to wed Coal," replied Domingo grimly.

"What about the other Maine Coon females? The ones that refuse to marry Coal?" asked Dusty.

"We're not 100 percent sure, but they may have been taken out of the country. The great king of the African realm told us some of his ape intelligence reported a caravan moving through the country of Nigeria. The apes reported a platoon of wildcats escorting a group of domestic cats fitting the description of the Maine Coons abducted."

"But why Africa?"

"I don't know, Dusty!" shouted Domingo. "Onc crisis at a time. We simply must solve the mission at hand before we start trying to launch an expedition to Africa."

"The question still stands, Captain! Why would a female Maine Coon agree to marry Coal?" asked Dusty.

"Some say she may have been swayed by promises of wealth, power, and all of the other things that tempt cats," said Domingo. "However, there is more. This information could be weeks or even months old. The first group of kittens may already be here. If that is the case, then they must be eliminated."

"I'm not an assassin!" shouted Dusty.

"For the sake of your new pride, you will kill or do anything else your king requires of you, half-breed." retorted Domingo.

"I have no earthly king!" shouted Dusty in response.

Domingo's expression grew softer. Walking over, he placed his paw gently on Dusty's shoulder. "Listen, Dusty. This thing has gone too far for us to back out now. If we fail in El Paso, not only will the cat race suffer but the humans as well. You know this to be true."

Dusty's face drew a grim frown. "I know, Captain," said Dusty.

"Then go!" commanded Domingo. "We have reports that a human truck company will be sending a truck to El Paso tonight around 12:00 p.m. Be at the overpass outside the zoo over I–26. We can't stop the truck, so you are going to have to jump."

"Great!" said Dusty with a noted tone of sarcasm. "Not only am I an assassin now, I also have to function as a bird."

Later at the overpass, Dusty intently stared at the traffic on I–26 illuminated by headlights. The spider-monkey escort was standing with him for support.

"Well!" said Dusty, addressing his escort. "Being an expert jumper, do you have any jumping tips?"

The spider monkey thought intently, looking at the traffic and calculating the distance from the bridge to the hard top. He wet his finger to get the direction of the wind and then did a quick calculation in his head.

"Just one tip," said the monkey. "Don't miss."

At first, Dusty grew angry at such a simple remark and then relaxed when he realized that the monkey's advice was sound and the best he had received all day.

"Here comes the truck!" shouted the spider monkey.

Dusty jumped up on the overpass railing. He could see the semi headlights growing larger as the truck grew closer.

"Wish me luck!" said Dusty, looking around at the spider monkey, but no one was there. Dusty quickly turned back around at the approaching truck. Dusty gauged his distance and then jumped. It seemed as though it took an eternity to fall. The sight of the pavement was suddenly blocked as the great semi moved under Dusty at great speed.

Thunk!

Dusty hit the top of the semi's trailer. He bounced to one side then was airborne again.

I'm falling off the top! thought Dusty. The roadway was coming up at him once again when suddenly, he stopped falling. The strap of his tote bag had caught on the jagged hooks mounted on top of the trailer. Breathing with relief, Dusty grabbed the strap of his tote bag and climbed back up on top of the trailer. Dusty laid on his back, waiting for his heart to finally slow down. The steady hum of the truck engine, along with the steady rumbling of the roadway, was like a wonderful lullaby to Dusty's tired body. His eyelids grew heavy as his thoughts drifted toward a name.

Lydia! he thought as he drifted off to sleep.

CONFLICT

Domingo found himself drifting toward the chambers of King Alfanso.

"What is it?" asked Alfanso as Domingo walked into the room.

"Forgive me, your grace, but something is bothering me."

"What is it, Captain?" asked Alfanso. "Did all go well with Sir Dusty launching out on the mission? He did not miss the truck, did he?"

"No, no, your grace. All has gone well!" said Domingo reassuringly. It's just one thing bothers me. Our focus has been too narrow. We are thinking about the cat kingdom, but what if Coal has enlisted others into his service?"

"What do you mean?" asked the king.

Domingo continued, "Let us just suppose, my lord, that Coal has eyes inside our realm. Word may have already reached him that we are on our way."

The king thought for a moment.

"You have a valid point, Captain. He would need not only ground forces but an air force as well."

"But that is impossible, my lord," replied Domingo. "All air power is loyal to you."

"Is it?" asked Alfanso, scratching his chin with his paw. "What manner of the bird family could possibly benefit from a trail of death that Coal could provide?"

Domingo grinned widely. "Without question, my king, it would be the buzzards."

"We just happen to have two here in the zoo, do we not?" asked the king.

Domingo saluted, anticipating his Kings request and ran from the royal chambers to his mission. An hour later, Domingo came back into the king's chambers with two buzzards dangling from his mouth.

"Ouch! You're killing me!" said one of the ugly birds.

"You're not dead yet, my friend. That depends on your response to my questions," replied Alfanso.

Domingo brought the birds to the feet of Alfanso and dropped the birds to the floor, his mouth dripping with saliva.

"Aaah, what a mess!" shouted the second bird. "Try a breath mint!"

"Silence!" shouted Domingo.

"Now," began Alfanso. "What shall we talk about? Oh, I know. How about Coal?"

"Coal? Coal?" asked one of the buzzards sheepishly. "I fail to see how a law-abiding bird would know anything about a cat."

"Hahahaha. Who said he was a cat?" responded Alfanso, walking closer to the ugly bird. "If you don't know anything about the name Coal, then how do you know Coal is a cat?"

The buzzards, with expressions of terror, looked at each other and swallowed with a giant gulp. Alfanso then walked over to the reluctant informant and gripped his head in his massive paw.

"Listen, you rotten boil," began Alfanso. "I have a representative of the Maine Coon kingdom, risking his life to stop the destruction of my realm, where—by the way—you dwell. He may succeed in doing just that, but not before I make your head into a pile of bird jam!" Lifting the bird to the ceiling and shaking him, Alfanso gave one more warning. "Sing, you buzzard!"

"Okay, okay," said the second bird. "Leo and I were to alert the local buzzard force once your guy started on his way."

"Domingo!" shouted Alfanso. "Alert Captain Hawk at once."

AIR WAR

Dawn was breaking through the Georgia sky when Dusty opened his eyes. He was still on top of the semi truck. Rubbing the sleep from his eyes, Dusty's vision became clear in time to see a sign that said Welcome to Statesboro, Georgia. Dusty had not been to Georgia since his birth so long ago. Suddenly, the hair raised on the back of Dusty's neck. As he turned around to see the source of this sensation, his world was unexpectedly rocked.

Pow!

Dusty found himself flying across the top of the truck. Shaking off the effects of the blow, Dusty looked up and saw the blue sky filled with black-winged figures, and they all appeared to be swooping down on him.

Thwap!

Dusty felt the talon rip into the flesh on his cheek. Dusty swung blindly at his attackers and hit one of the black birds, sending it over the edge of the semi.

Pow!

Dusty felt himself fly over the edge of the truck and saw the road coming up quick. Out of instinct, Dusty grabbed the top edge of the semi just in time.

"Aah!" shouted Dusty in pain as he gripped the truck for dear life.

"Finish him off!" shouted one of the buzzards as he flew overhead.

One of the dark-clad birds came swooping in low.

"You're done for, boy!" shouted the intruder as he closed in on his prey.

Dusty swung around, grabbing the edge of the trailer with his other paw. Swinging himself up on the truck again, Dusty dropped quickly on the roof just as a low-hanging tree limb passed overhead.

Ooof!

Dusty look behind him as the buzzard was silenced by the same low-hanging limb. The bird hung on the limb for only a moment and fell to the road. Dusty grabbed his tote bag and began swinging it over his head like a cowboy he saw on dad servant's television. The next buzzard came flying in low. *Thwap!* Dusty made contact with the tote bag, sending the buzzard flying over the cab of the truck in a hail of black feathers.

Voop!

Dusty felt the pain of yet another talon cutting the back of his head, sending him face down into the roof of the semi trailer.

"Oh," said Dusty as he rolled over to face the black sky, still stunned from the blow. The sky began to fill with more of the dark figures, increasing in size as they grew ever closer to Dusty. Lying helpless from his last massive blow, Dusty resolved himself to his fate.

"This is it, boys! Finish him off!" shouted the lead buzzard.

Just as one of the bird's talons were about to sink into Dusty's orange fur...*pow!* The bird exploded into a firework's show of black feathers. Looking up, Dusty saw a large red-tailed hawk hovering over him where the black buzzard once appeared. Then the sky was filled with air-to-air combat between buzzards and red-tailed hawks. Then Dusty's attention was drawn to a loud *thunk*. Looking beside him, he saw a massive red-tailed hawk that had landed on the truck next to him.

"Hello, mate," said the hawk. "Captain Jubal Hawk of King Alfanso's royal air force at your service."

"Thanks be to the Great One you showed up," said Dusty.

Dusty staggered slightly as he tried to get to his feet.

"Easy there, mate," said the hawk. "The buzzards were playing for keeps."

"Why are the birds involved?" asked Dusty. "I thought this was a struggle between cat and human."

"Not so, my orange friend," said Jubal. "If Coal is allowed to kill his enemies, the buzzards will eat quite well for a long time. Would you not agree?"

"That's it?" asked Dusty. "A square meal is all it took to get the buzzards on board?"

"Apparently," replied Jubal. "Makes you wonder if anyone else may be on the payroll. Does it not, lad?"

"So does that mean you're going to go with me the rest of the way?" asked Dusty with all the hope in his heart.

"Regrettably no, mate," replied Jubal. "We can fly cover for you until you reach the border of Alabama, and then you will be on your own again."

"But why?" asked Dusty.

"We are the South Carolina and Georgia hawks. Once we reach the border, we are out of our realm. By the king's law of the Americas, we can go no farther without the permission of the western king."

"Well, who would that be?" asked Dusty.

"Why, King Sancho, my lad," replied Jubal with a smile. "He is King Alfanso's brother. Guess they want to keep things in the family, eh?"

"But why can't you guys follow me all the way?" asked Dusty again, hoping for a different answer.

"Look, mate, my orders only allow me to escort you to the border. Beyond that, you're on your own. I'm sorry."

THE BODYGUARD

"Domingo!" shouted Alfanso.

"Yes, my lord," came the response.

"How did things go with the hawks?"

"All went well, my king," replied Domingo. "The hawks successfully defeated the dreaded buzzards, and our cat, Dusty, sustained minor injuries."

"Wonderful!" exclaimed Alfanso. "Have the hawks remained with Sir Dusty for the duration?"

"Impossible, my lord," replied Domingo. "It would be a clear violation of the boarder treaty you and your brother drew up."

Alfanso paused for a moment, scratching his chin.

"Does Sancho know anything about what is going on in El Paso?"

"Not from our sources, sir, but your brother has an extensive intelligence network of his own," replied Domingo.

"Then he may already know," said Alfanso. "Alert the falcon. I need the greatest of speed on this mission. Send word to Sancho that I need his help."

"And exactly what help would that be, my lord?"

"Dusty is going up against greater odds than we imagined," replied Alfanso. "He needs additional aid. Ask my brother in the dispatch to send his best soldiers to guard Dusty for the duration, and do explain the urgency of the situation. Make it so," commanded Alfanso.

As the falcon sped toward the realm of Sancho's kingdom, Dusty and the captain of the red-tailed hawks, Jubal, sat and talked on the top of the semi trailer as it moved toward the Alabama boarder.

"You seem disturbed, my friend," said Jubal.

"Uh, yeah!" replied Dusty. "A few days ago, I was an ordinary cat resting on the balcony of my mom and dad servant's home. Now I am here in the role of an assassin."

"You could use the help of a cat master," replied Jubal.

"Cat master?" asked Dusty.

"Yes! They are legendary cats of the forest. They are said to be able to defeat cats of every size in a fight."

"But where do you find a master?" asked Dusty.

Jubal laughed. "Why, Dusty, my lad, they are only legends. Their kind was said to have disappeared from sight hundreds of years ago."

"Why?" asked Dusty again, his fascination in full swing.

"No one knows," replied Jubal. "Oh, here it comes."

"What?" asked Dusty.

"The Alabama border of course."

"But how am I going to make it without help?" asked Dusty.

Jubal smiled. "Guess you better ask the Great Cat."

Jubal jumped and flew in the opposite direction of the semi.

"Fairwell, my friend!" shouted Jubal as he flew out of sight.

Dusty sat there by himself for a while, listening to the steady hum of the truck engines as it sped along. Looking up at the blue clear sky, Dusty thought, *Well, I have nothing to lose by giving him a shot.*

"I am told you are the Great One. All I know of you is what others have told me. I would like to know you myself. I could sure use some help here. If you will help me do what I need to do, Great Cat, then I promise I will serve you all the days of my life, if you would only show me how?"

Dusty suddenly felt sleepy, and the blue Alabama sky was growing steadily darker. He laid his back on the roof of the trailer and fell into a deep sleep.

THE WILD

Meanwhile, deep in the desert of El Paso, Texas, the sun drifted behind the mountains, and dusk started taking the heat from the surrounding sand. Only one animal trekked along the desert sand this evening. It was a cat of the Margay pride. He arrived at the base of a hill and began climbing. Halfway up the base of the large rock mountain, he paused at the entrance of the cave before going inside. The mysterious margay continued down the dark corridor toward a flickering firelight. The margay entered an open room illuminated by a campfire in one corner. A large broken mirror stood erect against the wall while a large dark cat groomed himself in front of it.

"Has all gone well with the attack?" asked the dark cat.

The margay quickly bowed before responding to the dark cat's question.

"Not as well as we had hoped, my lord."

"What!" screamed the black cat as he quickly turned toward the margay still bowed on the floor of the cave.

"Get up, get up, Major," commanded the black cat. "Full report at once!"

The large dark cat was now fully illuminated by the firelight, revealing him to be a black panther.

"My lord, we have a leak in our air force," said the margay as he rose to his feet.

"It figures!" replied the panther. "Never trust a bird to do cat's job."

"Yes, my Lord Coal. I agree." said the margay.

"It is obvious that everything is now known," said Coal. "There is now no reason for stealth, at least from the animal kingdom. Those who betray me must suffer for their lack of vision. Send word to my assassin in the Riverbanks Zoo to take care of this problem. Plug the leak."

"It shall be done, my lord Coal."

At that time, a beautiful black Maine Coon walked into the room.

"Oh, my dear Fortune. Is all well with my kittens?" asked Coal.

"Yes, yes, my lord," replied Fortune as she came into the light. "They show remarkable progress in their speaking, reading, and hunting skills."

"Excellent!" shouted Coal. "If you will excuse us, my dear, the major and I have a great deal to talk about."

"Why, yes, my lord," replied Fortune in a nervous voice. "I do beg your pardon."

"No need, my pet. We shall talk later," replied Coal.

Fortune bowed, leaving the room.

"Ah, what a beauty! Too bad I will have no further need for her once the kittens come of age," said Coal.

"About the infiltrator, sir?" asked the major.

"Oh yes, Major Thorn. What do we know about this one-cat army they are sending to stop me?"

"Well my lord, our intelligence tells us he goes by the name Dusty."

Coal laughed hysterically. "That figures," said Coal in between breaths.

"Yes, my lord, we have been informed that his mother was a princess of the Savannah realm called Abercorn."

"And his father?" asked Coal.

"Well, my lord, we have no records of his father at all."

"No records?" asked Coal. "Why would there be no records?"

"I am a soldier, my lord, not a scribe. So I fear I cannot give you a logical answer," replied Major Thorn.

"Well, the answer is elementary, my dear Thorn. You and your intelligence network is looking in the wrong place. If you can't find the answer among the domestic cat records, then you may want to consider looking among the wildcat records."

"Impossible, my lord!" replied Thorn.

"Is it?" asked Coal. "Do not be too confident that we are the only ones to think of crossing breeds to enhance special abilities, Thorn. Check it out."

"Yes, sir," replied Thorn.

"If my suspicion is correct, then this Dusty is indeed someone of importance. No matter. He is far too late to stop me now. The kittens are already here, and my plan already is sprouting like a desert rose."

"Do not let us forget, my lord, he did manage to stop the air attack long enough to get re-enforcements," replied Thorn.

"Yes, he did!" replied Coal. "I am beginning to think that you think he has some special training or abilities, Major?"

"Abilities are likely, my lord, if your suspicion of his father rings true. Training is doubtful, my lord. Our reports have him just being hired by the Great Cat Council, and it takes me at least three months to train a cat soldier in just the basic arts of war."

"It matters not!" said Coal. "He must be eliminated before he receives additional help or training. Tell me, Major, are you aware of the legend of the cat masters?"

"Why, yes, my lord. I am."

"Really?" asked Coal. "Then please fill me in on this illusive story. For all of my education, I seem to be lacking in this one area of history, and it intrigues me."

Thorn cleared his throat and began.

"Well, my lord Coal, the first of the cat masters was called one. It is said that the masters abandoned ordinary names to diminish the risk of unnecessary pride. One was served by a Chinese human in the Americas in the cat year 1810. It was said this human servant of One was very skilled in the art of fighting. One spent hours watching his servant practice his art. Through his observation, he developed a cat style of fighting we know today as paw. In time, One's servant had a wife and cubs of his own. As the human cubs grew, their father taught them to read Chinese as well as the new language—English, which is spoken by our servants today. The legend claims that One actually learned the languages himself though I don't see how or why. We know there is no more complicated language than *Catdomnese*.

"In his old age, he left the house of his servants and sought an apprentice to pass his teachings. Of course, my lord, that is where the legend ends. There have been stories over the last couple of centuries of cats doing amazing things, but nothing truly recorded or confirmed."

"So, you don't feel there is any possible way that a cat master could exist today?" asked Coal.

"Given the historical facts, my lord, I would say no. Even if one did exist, his vows would not allow him to kill a wildcat," replied Thorn.

"Why is that, Major?"

"Specifically why we are not sure, my lord, but I can only assume a wildcat helped the masters at one time," replied Thorn.

"Very well then," replied Coal. "I can rest assured that this Dusty is not properly trained and certainly, hahaha, not part of this legendary cat master pride. So send out five of your best cat soldiers. I want him killed at the Mississippi. Oh, by the way, Thorn, what type of cat were the masters reported as being?"

"The only species the legend reports is the species One was a part of, my lord. A strange breed known as the Norwegian Forest Cats.

MISSISSIPPI CAT FIGHT

Dusty was sleeping in peaceful slumber as the semi trailer trekked along the countryside. It had been hours since his conversation with the Great One. Dusty struggled to open his eyes and bring them into focus. The blue sky managed to clear with beautiful clouds flying softly by. Dusty rolled over on his side just in time to see the Welcome to Mississippi sign pass by on the side of the road. The Mississippi river looked muddy as the truck sped over the bridge.

Dusty stood up and stretched out his arms to release his tensed muscles when suddenly, he felt something grab his paw. A rope wrapped round and round his paw. Dusty saw the rope leading from his paw, off the side of the semi, and into the top of a pine tree. As the truck passed by, the tree began to look smaller, and the slack in the rope became taut. Suddenly, there was no more slack, and Dusty was catapulted off the top of the truck into a nearby wood line.

Everything went black. Dusty felt terrible pain in the top of his head. His eyes opened slowly to see the canopy of tall rising trees in a forest. The rope that gripped him earlier was still wrapped around his paw, rising up a nearby tree trunk and vanishing into the top of the canopy. Picking himself slowly off the forest floor, Dusty unwrapped the rope from his paw. He licked the rope burn around his paw and rubbed his now-injured shoulder muscle.

"I thought assassins fared better in such matters," came a voice from the forest.

Dusty turned toward the sound of the mysterious voice, revealing a margay cat.

"Who are you? And what do you want?" demanded Dusty.

"First of all, my friend, it is not what I want but what we want," said the margay.

At that moment, four more margay cats emerged from the forest thicket, surrounding Dusty.

"As far as my name is concerned, assassin, you may call me Blade. It will be the last name you ever hear."

"*Raaaaaaaaaah!*" came a shriek, echoing through the forest. Four of the margay cats turned with Dusty to see the empty spot where one of their group had stood. Blade peered into the dark forest seeing nothing.

"Sergeant? Sergeant, where are you?" asked Blade.

There was no reply.

"Aaaaaah!" came another scream. All the cats turned, only to find there were now only three of them remaining.

"Hook? Private Hook? Sergeant? Where are you?" shouted Blade. Dusty gasped slightly as he saw two dim green eyes appear near a dark tree stump and then disappear.

"What did you see?" demanded Blade, grabbing Dusty by the throat.

"Ooooof!" came another scream. Now the group had only two cats remaining.

"Who are you?" shouted Blade. "What do you want?"

"Raaaaah!" came another scream. Spinning around, Blade saw that only Dusty and he remained. Dusty looked quickly in all directions and then realized that he was the only cat in the forest.

He could feel his heart racing. Panic began to set in. He couldn't speak. Dusty felt the hair rose on the back of his neck. Whatever made the cats disappear was now behind him. Dusty was shaking from head to paw, but he knew he had to turn around. Slowly, he turned, his heart beating faster and faster. He could hardly breathe. There, sitting on a rock was a cat unlike any he had ever seen before. The cat was a colorful blend of black, gray, and charcoal. His eyes were like green fire, and he had a beautiful gold medallion hanging from his neck with the number seven etched inside.

Dusty stood still, not knowing if he should run or faint as the mysterious cat looked him over from head to toe.

"You don't seem to be much of a threat to Coal, young one," said the mysterious cat. "Apparently, Coal has not seen you." The mysterious cat laughed joyfully. "This is wonderful."

"What? Uh, why?" replied Dusty, very confused by this statement.

"Like many cats of the wild, Dusty, they tend to look on the outward appearance," began the mysterious cat. "They are blind to the attributes within a cat. In hunting, they do not look for those that appear to be strong; rather they tend to seek those that appear to be weak. Of all the weaknesses of wildcats, this is their greatest one."

"How do you know my name? How do you know Coal?" asked Dusty.

"How I know, son of Juno, is not quite as important. What is more important is that you need to help, son of Juno."

"Who is Juno?" asked Dusty.

"Your father, of course," replied the mysterious cat.

Dusty was in shock. He never knew the name of his father, and he sure did not know this strange cat giving him this information.

"Thank you for saving my life, sir. May I ask what your name may be?" asked Dusty.

"My name is Seven, young cat, but you have not earned the right to call me by that name."

Dusty was rather taken aback by such bluntness from a stranger, but he did owe this cat his very life.

"Very well then, how do I address you, sir?"

"You may call me master or teacher. That will show the proper respect from a student," replied Seven.

Dusty again was shocked by this old cat's statements but tried to maintain his composure.

"Very well, Master. I would love to stay and chat, but I have a mission, and I am not sure how I am going to get to El Paso now that my ride is far up the road."

"Well, then, are you too proud to accept help?" asked Seven.

"Why no, Master." replied Dusty.

"Then the first step toward success is being humble enough to accept and admit you don't know everything," began Master Seven. "You have taken that step, and you are now one step closer to completing your mission."

"I don't know about all of that, Master, but I do need help in getting to El Paso and quickly. I fear that more attacks are coming, and I don't think I have what it takes to defeat one cat, much less five wildcats as you have obviously done. May I ask, what did you do with them?"

"Why, they are very much alive, my friend. I am going to allow them to hang around while we continue our conversation back at my lair."

Out of instinct, Dusty look up toward the canopy of the forest and, there, hanging in the treetops were the five wildcats, bound by ropes and gagged, not making a sound.

"I am greatly surprised that King Alfanso was able to send help so quickly," said Dusty, fishing for information.

"Oh, I assure you, my young student, that he was unable to do so," replied Seven. "If he had, then there would have been no need for me to be here."

"I don't understand!" replied Dusty, totally confused by the statement. "If Alfanso did not send you, then how did you know I needed help? How did you know my name? More important, Master, how were you able to take out five wildcats in such a short time?"

"Ah, how is it, young cat, that you were unable to do so yourself?" replied the mysterious Seven.

Dusty felt he already knew the answer to that question. The more Dusty found out, the less he was really aware.

Seven looked about the forest, raising his nose and smelling the slight breeze as it traveled through the leaves.

"We must get indoors. The cats of the wild rarely hunt in small numbers like these, and it is likely they had backup nearby. Come with me, and stay quiet. I will let you know when it is safe to talk again."

Dusty followed the strange cat into the thick, dark woods of Mississippi as darkness began to fall onto parts yet unknown.

THE TRAINER

Domingo entered King Alfanso's chambers around midnight.

"Yes, Captain? What is it?"

"A report from King Sancho, my lord," replied Domingo. "His troopers came upon a scene in the Mississippi forest that has more questions than answers. One of Sancho's falcons reported seeing Dusty pulled from the top of the truck he was traveling on. Then Sancho's other forces picked up wild-cat prints in the forest near the abduction. There were visible signs of a struggle, but nothing was found. Nothing, that is, except four margay cats hanging in the forest trees bound and gagged."

"Really?" asked Alfanso. "Perhaps Dusty is a much better fighter than we anticipated."

"I don't think so, my lord," replied Domingo. "We found signs of not one but two sets of paw prints leading into the forest, but we quickly lost sight of the trail.

Most odd. It takes someone very special and very skilled to hide their trail from King Sancho's soldiers."

"So you just gave up, Captain?" demanded Alfanso.

"My lord, this was enemy territory, and Sancho's troopers were themselves being tracked by Coal's forces."

Alfanso's expression softened. "Yes, you are quite right, Captain. I forget you were not personally there to lead. My apologies. It is just this entire situation is wearing thin on my nerves."

"No need, your grace," replied Domingo.

"The paw prints...were they wild or domestic prints?" asked Alfanso.

"Why, they were domestic, your grace."

"Smashing!" shouted Alfanso.

"I don't think I understand, my lord."

"This means he is still alive, Captain. Don't you see?"

"But what of the other set of prints, my lord."

"Who cares!" replied Alfanso. Coal, as far as we know, has mostly wildcats working for him and only a few domestics. In this case, as we well know, only a domestic cat will help another domestic cat. That means we have a 95 percent chance of still being in business. Send word to the falcons to continue the search for Dusty and bring me word as soon as they pick up his trail. And oh yes, get clearance from my brother to work in cooperation with his air force."

"By your command!" replied Domingo as he bowed.

STILL IN MISSISSIPPI

Meanwhile, in the Mississippi forest, sunlight entered through the thick forest canopy into a clearing. In the center of the clearing stood a large thatch hut. Underneath the shelter, a warm fire crackled, and straw pillows formed comfortable chairs all around.

Fram!

The sound broke the silence of the forest as Dusty landed on his back in the center of the shelter floor.

"Your attack was no more a threat than that of a clumsy cub," said Seven in an amused voice. "Get up and try again."

"Master!" began Dusty. "Can I take a break? My back is killing me."

"So will Coal!" replied Seven. "Do you think he will show mercy when you are on your back in front of him?"

"Master, there is no way for me to become as proficient as you before Coal arrives," said Dusty in a worried voice.

"True!" said Seven. "But you only need to master one throw in order to defeat him."

"Why me, Master?" asked Dusty.

"Why not you?" asked Seven. "Who are we to question the motives of the Great One? He chooses those cats he wishes. In doing so, they gain wisdom."

"Well, what do you do with the wisdom once you have acquired it?" asked Dusty as he lifted himself from the shelter floor and licked his sore paws.

"For the first time, you really begin to live and see the Great One for who he really is," replied Seven.

Dusty scratched his head and pondered what his new-found teacher was saying.

"What is going to happen with Coal, Master Seven?"

"Coal is bent on conquest of the cat and human races," began Seven. Humans are fearful of wildcats and would never attempt to serve them. Coal knows the only way he can do this is by having a wildcat that looks like a domestic cat. The Maine Coons are the perfect choice. The human servants refer to them as the *gentle giants*."

"Why?" asked Dusty.

Seven walked over to his desk in the corner and pulled a paper from the center drawer.

"Look at this, Dusty, and tell me what you think?" said Seven.

Dusty took the paper and began to read.

"New York Times, October 30, 1996."

Unusual! thought Dusty.

Then he realized that he just read human writing. In fact, he had been reading human writing his entire trip and had only now realized this.

"I can read human."

"Yes, you can," replied Seven. "You and every other Maine Coon. No other cat has this gift. The Maine

Coons have kept this secret for centuries. Coal knew there was a great secret among the cat races, but he was unsure what race of cats held the secret. So he captured and interrogated numerous cats until one, a Maine Coon, told him what he wanted to know. Cats that can read human writing would be unstoppable in the hands of a mad wildcat. A cat that is wild and a Maine Coon would be a threat to cats and humans alike."

Dusty lowered his head.

"Master, King Alfanso wants me to kill the kittens of Coal, if they are already born."

"Yes, I know," replied Seven.

"Then what do I need to do?" asked Dusty.

"That which is right," replied Seven. "In doing so, you will find your path or forever lose it by doing the wrong thing. Think of the power a cat would have if he were able to speak all cat languages, human, English, and read the English language. A cat like that in the paws of Coal could destroy cat civilization as we now know it."

"Or bring it closer together in the hands of another?" asked Dusty.

"Aah!" replied Seven. "Now you begin to see. Should our concern be the path by which one enters the Great One's world, or should our concern be with the shaping of that life once it is here? Water, my young student, can either bring life or death depending on what environment you bring it into. Water in a bowl given to a thirsty cat can give life. Water in the same cat's nose and lungs brings death."

"But, Master, these kittens are totally different."

"No!" shouted Seven. "No cat coming into this human world is by accident, for life comes from the Great One—the great cat called Judah. Each cat has purpose, has worth, and has a mission that no other cat can do. Why? Because it is that cat's mission to fulfill, his to complete. Some cats become great leaders, kings, soldiers, pride governors, and cat doctors. Just suppose one of the kittens you kill is the one cat that has been given to our world to unlock various cures for many of the sicknesses that kill our kind? What then, my young student? Who will then accomplish his purpose? I tell you no one! For it was his to fulfill."

Dusty found himself speechless.

"Ponder these things, my young apprentice," replied Seven. "But as you do, let us try the throw again and, this time, with feeling."

"With feeling?" asked Dusty. "The only feelings I have are from bumps and bruises."

"You must feel the movement of your opponent. When darkness is the only light you have to fight by, then feeling and the shift of air are the only allies you have. Now let us begin."

Seven took his stance in the center of the room as Dusty once again made his approach.

THE CHILDREN

Meanwhile, back at the dark cave of Coal, his loyal major, Thorn, brought him his usual report. Thorn approached and bowed his head.

"Yes, Thorn. What is it?" asked Coal.

"My lord, it would appear that that idiot Blade failed to capture the assassin."

"What?" shouted Coal.

"Yes, my lord, it is true," replied Thorn, already feeling the grip of his master's paw on his throat. "They were obviously overpowered by a much superior force, yet only the footprints of a domestic cat were found in the forest."

"Indeed?" replied Coal. "It would appear that this Dusty is indeed a much superior fighter than I gave him credit for being. If he can take out my best cats by himself, then he is indeed a great threat to our ultimate goals."

"I agree, my lord," replied Thorn. "That being said, my lord, what then shall we do?"

"Isn't it obvious, my dear Thorn? We go to war."

"But with whom do we fight, my lord?" asked Thorn.

"No one but King Alfanso and his army."

"He could not possibly assemble his army in time to meet us on the field of battle without the whole human race being alerted."

"Yes, you are quite right, my lord Coal! But who is to say we will be going up against Alfanso, my lord?"

"What do you mean, Thorn?"

"As you say, my lord, Alfanso cannot possibly go up against us, and Dusty cannot possibly defeat us by himself. And let us not forget that Sancho, Alfanso's brother, cannot interfere without alerting the human populous as you have said. The rules of engagement state that every king must lead his own army, and his absence from the El Paso zoo would raise questions to say the least. So the only logical conclusion is that Dusty must have some sort of army awaiting to help him."

Coal looked thoughtfully out his bedroom window, overlooking the El Paso desert.

"Yes, you are quite right, Thorn. We need to get word to this young warrior that we will meet him on the field of battle."

"But to what end, my lord? asked Thorn.

"The children must be saved, Thorn. They are still kittens but will soon be at the age we can begin their training. If we wait, this Dusty might, however unlikely, sneak his way into our lair and somehow steal or kill them. If those cats fall into Alfanso's hands, they could be used to forever stop any further attempts at ruling man and animal kind. We must lure them into an all-out war—a winner-take-all proposition."

"But the children will be safely evacuated while the fighting is going on. Correct, my lord?"

"Correct, Thorn. Apparently being around my genius is influencing your own intellect. Now let us carefully draft a letter of war. When it is complete, we will contact one of the falcons from Sancho's air force and have our emissary taken to Dusty with the finished declaration."

"As you wish, my lord," replied Major Thorn as he turned and made his way down the dark corridor, busy with his new task.

A RUMOR OF WAR

Dusty was nervous. With a blindfold over his eyes, he had only his hearing to aid him. *Swoosh!* An arrow headed straight for his head.

Swack!

Dusty swatted the projectile with his paw.

Swoosh, Swoosh!

Dusty moved to one side, allowing one arrow to miss him as he caught the other arrow with his paw.

"Good!" says Seven. "Take the blindfold off."

Dusty took off his blindfold after dropping the arrow to the ground. Suddenly his vision came into focus. He saw Seven place his bow and arrow in the corner of the room.

"You seem to have a natural affinity for avoiding projectiles, Dusty. This will serve you well," said Seven.

Dusty walked to the edge of the thatched structure and listened intently. "Master, something is different in the forest this evening," said Dusty.

"Yes, and how would you describe it, my young student?"

"It is as if everyone in the forest knows something evil is moving about."

"Yes, my young apprentice," said Seven. "It takes a discerning spirit to see evil while it is taking place. That which is good will move away from it, if it has any wisdom at all. Thus we hear silence in the forest tonight."

"What do you mean by that, Master?" asked Dusty. "Do you mean that evil is approaching the forest as we speak?"

"No, my young student," said Seven. "Evil is now upon us."

Seven pointed to the corner of the thatched structure, and at the entrance to the structure stood a dark figure of a black cat holding a scroll in his paw. Dusty silently caught his breath at the sight of the obviously domestic yet evil cat.

"Greetings, Dusty of Columbia, most worthy foe of Coal, future ruler of the known world," said the dark figure with ceremony and yet contempt.

"Come into the light of the fireplace, black cat," said Seven.

The dark cat stepped into the light, revealing not a domestic cat, but rather a rare, almost black, American bobcat.

"Your name, black evil?" demanded Seven.

"I am Cain. Servant of Coal."

"State your business, you evil wildcat, or be gone with you. We have not the time or inclination for foolishness," shouted Seven.

"No one speaks to me that way!" shouted the bobcat.

The vicious bobcat screamed like a human female as he swung his claw toward Seven's face. Grabbing the cat by the wrist, Seven turned the cat's wrist slightly as a crack snapped out into the room. The bobcat fell to the floor, paralyzed in his attack position. He was stiff as a board, his facial expression still intact, yet still very much alive. Dusty looked at Seven with astonishment.

"Oh, don't worry, my young student. The effects of this particular move are temporary. However, he will never regain full use of that arm."

"That's kind of cruel, would you not say, Master?" asked Dusty.

"I would not, my young trainee. What is worse is his death or losing some mobility in that arm?" asked Seven sternly.

"You have made your point, Master," replied Dusty, ashamed once again that he dare question his master's motives.

Seven tapped the end of the paper scroll, and it flew up into his paw. Seven handed the scroll to Dusty.

"I believe this belongs to you, Dusty. Read it, and let us deduce the motives of our enemy."

When Dusty opened the scroll, Seven reached down with his toe pad and tapped the black cat behind the ear. The black cat went limp and fell into a deep sleep.

"How did you do that, Master?"

"In due time, my student," replied Seven. "Now the scroll?"

Dusty opened the scroll and began to read.

> To my most worthy opponent.
>
> First and foremost I congratulate you on making it this far on your very long journey. However, you want what I have, and I in turn cannot give you what you want. There is no further need for the innocent to be injured. Let the soldiers end this conflict. We will meet you on the desert of El Paso. The victors will have the prize.
>
> Coal

"Interesting!" said Seven.

— 80 —

"Why, Master? We are in Mississippi. El Paso is very far away, and we are no closer to finding the kittens than when we began. It would appear that we are not advancing much at all, Master," said Dusty.

"So sure are you?" said Seven. "South Carolina is much farther from El Paso, and Mississippi is much closer. So geographically we seem to be making advances."

"Wow, you sure are a 'glass is half full' kind of cat, Master," replied Dusty.

"Do you believe Coal?" asked Seven.

"Why no, Master. He is a villain, and as you have told me in the short time I have known you, 'There is no honor among thieves.'"

"True enough!" said Seven. "But you must also look to half truths.

Dusty's obvious puzzled looked said everything to Seven.

"Coal wants a battle," began Seven. "That we can deduce rather easily. But why would he want one when he could simply try and slip away? He says the prize will be the kittens, yet he offers no proof that the kittens do in fact exist. However, we can conclude they do exist because he mentions them in an offhanded way. So what does this villain not tell us?"

"Well," began Dusty. "He does not tell us how we get the kittens if we win."

"Correct!" shouted Seven, thrilled Dusty came to the right conclusion. "What does that bit of information tell you, Dusty?" asked Seven.

"The kittens are not going to be the prize because they will not be present," replied Dusty. "The battle will only be a decoy for Coal to escape with the kittens."

"Exactly right," said Seven.

Seven took a clam shell from a small nail on the main shelter's pillar. As he blew the horn with all of his might, a long melodious song rang throughout the forest.

"What was that for, Master?" asked Dusty.

"We are gathering our troops, Dusty," replied the mysterious Seven. "Something is about to be done here tonight that has not been done in one hundred years."

Suddenly a red-tailed falcon landed at the entrance of Seven's abode.

"I heard your call, Master," replied the bird. "How may I serve you?"

"Sergeant!" replied Seven. "Get ready to take a message to King Alfanso by way of his brother Sancho. War is at hand. Commit these instructions to memory and then make haste."

WAR IS AT HAND

Alfanso looked out of his zoo cage as the sun began to go down behind the beautiful Columbia wood line. A great deal of red beef sat in his dish where it had gone untouched for over an hour. Domingo could not remember a time when the king let food go bad. Even when the king was sick, he always had something to eat. Domingo cleared his throat to alert his king to his presence.

"Ahem."

"Ah, yes, Captain. What is it?"

"My king, is there something wrong?" asked Domingo. "I could not help but notice that you have not touched your food. Are you all right, my lord?"

"Not really, Captain," replied Alfanso. "We have not heard from our cat, Dusty, for some time. If I were outside the walls of this zoo, I would not feel so helpless."

"What exactly are you fearful of, my lord?" inquired Domingo.

"Coal, Captain. That is what I am afraid of. If Dusty fails to retrieve those kittens, life as we know it will end. Cats throughout history have always been free and powerful as long as humans were allowed to serve us. If Coal's plan succeeds, then life as we know it ends. The humans who feed and serve us will either fall outright, or they will in turn begin to see what is going on and fear us. They will then turn from being servants to being our killers. Domestic breeds will suffer the most, and all knowledge of the Great One could be suppressed for all time."

"Why would he want to do that, sir?" asked Domingo.

"Without law, my friend Domingo, then there is no knowledge of wrongdoing. Mark my words, Coal would stop at nothing to justify himself, and doing away with any knowledge of the Great One's law would suit him well."

"I tend to believe the power of the Lion of Judah is much more powerful than a panther in El Paso, my lord," said Domingo.

Alfanso forced a sick grin.

"Yes, Captain. You put me to shame."

Suddenly, a spider monkey entered the room.

"My king!" shouted the spider monkey.

"Yes, yes, Corporal. Tell me while I am still young," retorted Alfanso as he grabbed his forehead.

"Sergeant Sky of King Sancho's air force whishes to speak with you."

"Well, don't just stand there, you dirty ape. Show him in!" shouted Domingo.

The monkey escorted the red falcon into the room and left.

"Sergeant Sky of King Sancho's royal air force, my king."

"You are most welcome, Sergeant. Do you have word of our cat Dusty?" asked Alfanso.

"Yes, I do, my lord," replied Sky. "He is well. But I don't bring word exactly from your brother, my lord. I also serve another."

"Who then?" asked Alfanso as his voice cracked in fear.

"I serve the master of an organization known only to legend, an organization to which Sir Dusty now belongs," replied Sky.

"What organization?" asked Domingo sheepishly.

"The masters, my lord," answered Sky. "The legendary cat masters. They do exist, and they are in need of aid."

Alfanso and Domingo stood motionless in the room, their mouths fully extended.

"Did you hear what I said, my king?" asked the falcon, concerned by the silence.

"Y...y...yes, Sergeant. I did," replied Alfanso, reaching over and closing Domingo's mouth gently. "So what is the message?"

"We are at war, my lord," replied the falcon. "The treasonous Coal has declared war on the region of your brother Sancho. By cat law, he must act but cannot due to the human populous gaining suspicion. It is for this reason the cat masters have broken with their anonymity at least for now and come forward to fight so all other cat kingdoms can remain in place and so our human servants can remain ignorant of this episode in our history. Your brother, Sancho, has his forces surrounding the perimeter of the region, where the battle is to take place. No one will be able to enter or leave. His domestic and wildcat forces should be able to take shifts guarding this area day and night, but they are under strict orders not to engage. The cat masters made it very clear that they are the only forces to engage. The top cat master, known as Seven, requested that you send your air force and the two great eagles of Columbia to aid in this conflict."

"Of course!" shouted Alfanso. "All of us will go and win this fight."

"No, no, my lord," responded Sergeant Sky. "If the humans see the entire zoo empty and countless wildlife all starting to head toward El Paso, then the cat's carefully held secrets could be revealed."

Alfanso stopped himself.

"Yes, of course, Sergeant. I must be mad!" replied Alfanso. "Very well. Domingo!"

"Sir," replied Domingo.

"Alert the air force. Also, alert my domestic cats living in my brother's region to join my brother's forces. And have one of our cranes fly to the Savannah River tonight and alert the two great eagles and brief them on the mission."

"By your command!" shouted Domingo as he raced out of the room.

THE RACE FOR EL PASO

Dusty stood at the opening of Seven's abode, looking into the darkness. Just waiting and waiting—waiting for what exactly he did not know, for his elusive master did not tell him.

"The answer to your questions are out there in the darkness, my apprentice?" asked Seven.

"I was hoping you could tell me, Master. I am so nervous and scared I can hardly keep a thought in my head."

"Fear does not come from the Great One. So therefore, it must come from somewhere else," replied Seven.

"Yes, Master. You are right," replied Dusty. "So how do I control fear?" he asked.

"Fear is not something you control, my young student. Rather you control your own actions in spite of the fear. Love, for example, is not a feeling nor is it something you *fall into*. Love is an act of the will. You choose to love, and likewise, you can choose to act in spite of being fearful. It requires action, not feeling."

"But, Master, we do in fact feel these emotions," said Dusty.

"You must think of this in terms of three cats following each other. The first cat is named Fact. The second cat is named Faith. The third cat is named Feeling. If you concentrate on what is factual and place your faith in that fact, then your feelings will eventually catch up with you, my young student."

"But thus the question still stands, Master. How do I control fear at this moment until I can get good at what you have just told me?"

"Fair enough," said Seven. "Fear, my boy, is the result of the absence of trust in something or someone. All cats, if they acknowledge it or not, either draw or reject their strength from the Great One, that large Lion of Judah. The more you get to know this Great Cat, the more you trust him to take care of you. Thus, your fear will diminish."

"But how can I trust a cat I have never seen?" asked Dusty.

"By looking at all the trials he has already brought you through," replied Seven. "That is how trust is established. The Great One has guided you from birth to this moment. He has earned the right to be trustworthy. So the question for you, my young student, is do you trust him to take you the rest of the way?"

As Dusty pondered the wisdom of his master teacher, he heard the sound of feet walking in the darkness of the forest. Closer, the steps came to the entrance of the shelter.

"Master?" shouted Dusty.

"Yes, I know, my boy," replied Seven with a reassuring tone. "I hear them. Allow them to enter."

Who? thought Dusty as the steps got closer. Dusty stepped back from the entrance of the shelter as Seven approached. Then, appearing in the light was a very handsome bobcat wearing a necklace like his master's.

"Greetings, Master Seven," said the bobcat as he bowed.

"You are most welcome, Master Twenty-three," said Seven.

Then another cat appeared. This time, it was an orange calico wearing the same type necklace.

"Greetings, Master Seven," said the calico.

"You are welcome, Master Eighteen," replied Seven.

And on this ritual continued. Cat after cat appeared, Calicos, Tabbies, Bobcats, Norwegian Forest Cats, Maine Coons, Mountain lions, and Himalayan Persians. The variety continued, all wearing the same type necklace, and all being greeted by Seven with a number. Soon the shelter was filled with cats from every breed, size, and shape, and when all of them could no longer fit under the massive shelter, they surrounded the shelter holding glowing torches.

Then, a black domestic Shorthair stepped up in the midst of the crowd and, holding his paws high, gave the signal for the crowd to stop talking and socializing.

"Hear ye, hear ye!" shouted the domestic Shorthair "All having business with the assembly of masters come forth, and you shall be heard. The honored master known as Seven now presides."

The black domestic Shorthair bowed and backed reverently into the crowd as Seven approached and stood in a chair so all could see him.

"My fellow masters, all of these years since the beginning with our founder, Master One, we have sought to bring peace and unity among the cat races and to protect the humans so lovingly serving us. Now we have one of our own that would destroy all that we have worked and suffered so long to accomplish. The panther Coal is now assembling his army at the desert of El Paso. He proposes a winner-take-all approach to this needless conflict."

A mountain lion stepped forward and began to speak.

"But even that seems out of our paws, Master Seven. Even if we go through with this, as I know we must, the code forbids us from killing a fellow wildcat."

Talking and whispers emerged through the crowd. Seven raised his hand, and the crowd became silent again.

"You are quite right, Master Twelve," replied Seven. "But the laws and traditions written for the masters were written in a time of peace. We cannot afford to be so bound by traditions that it overrides good common sense. If Coal is not stopped, then all that the masters have promised to protect will be in jeopardy."

The crowd once again erupted into talking. Master Twelve once again stepped forward, and the crowd began to subside with its talking.

"You are quite right, Master Seven. Coal may not offer us a choice other than to kill him. But is there no other way to preserve this tradition?"

"Yes, there is," replied Seven. "Dusty!"

Dusty made his way through the crowd to the center of the room, where Seven stood on the chair.

"This is Dusty," began Seven. "Son of Custard, princess of the Savannah realm called Abercorn. And he is also son of Juno, prince of Savannah bobcats."

The crown exploded with chatter. There were shouts, gasps, and whispers.

"Quiet!" shouted the black shorthair. "Order! Order!"

The crowd fell quiet. Seven began once again.

"Never has such a mix in breeds happened before, but it would appear that the Great One knows better than we do."

"But he is a half-breed," shouted one cat in the crowd.

"So what!" shouted Seven with a voice of anger that brought absolute silence to the room.

You could have heard a pin drop on the dirt floor of the shelter as all eyes were fixed on Seven. Seven surveyed the crowd with an angry brow, and then his expression softened once again.

"He is a cat," said Seven. "A living, breathing, gifted member of the cat community created to and for that great Lion of Judah whom you all serve. Can any of you serve the intent of the Great One if you reject any one of the instruments he has provided for you to work with?"

Once again, there was silence in the room.

"Behold!" said Seven, pointing to Dusty. "An instrument of the Great Lion. He is part wild, so he has the abilities of a wildcat, and he is a domestic Maine Coon, possessing all the attributes of that race of cat. No one here is as equipped for the task at hand and the code of the Masters, though mentioning wildcats does not address the uniqueness of a mixed cat. Now I am done speaking. Does anyone have anything else to say before we begin?"

The crowd was silent.

"Very well," began Seven. "Gather around, and we will talk about our strategy for this battle."

WAR IS BREWING

The desert floor could not be seen because wildcats of every kind covered the area below the mountain of Coal—Mountain lions, Margays, Bobcats, and Domestic Wildcats like Calicos and Tabbies, who joined Coal's ranks after being abandoned by their human servants.

The crowd waited patiently for their elusive leader as they chatted among themselves. Meanwhile, as the crowd waited, high in his waiting room cave, Coal prepared himself as cat servants brushed his fur, shined his claws, and sprayed him with favorable perfume.

"*Meeeh-aw! Meeeh-aw!*" said Coal, looking at himself in the half-broken mirror as he stroked his whiskers in approval.

"You look most smashing, my lord," said Major Thorn.

"Smashing? Yes, yes, Major. I do agree with you. Nothing else would do for a ruler of the known cat world."

The sound of the crowd of wildcats rose from below Coal's window so he could hear it plainly.

"If you are almost ready, my lord, the crowd awaits your address!" said Thorn with an air of excitement.

One of the servants placed a purple cape on Coal's shoulders and clipped it in place with a golden chain. Then another servant placed a gold crown of fig leaves upon Coal's head. Coal gazed longingly at himself in the mirror, stroked his whiskers one more time, and then moved toward the balcony.

"How do I look, Thorn?"

"Kingly, my lord. Most kingly."

"Well said, Major," replied Coal as they walked out on the balcony in full view of the crowd.

The crowd went wild with excitement as their leader came into view high above them on the balcony. Coal held his paw up in approval as to soak up the cheers coming from his army. Major Thorn stepped forward, holding up both paws, and the crowd's screams died down to silence. Coal cleared his throat and began his speech.

"My fellow wildcats, today we unite for the first time under one unified command—yours truly."

Again the crowd went wild. Coal raised his paw, and the crowd again quieted their enthusiasm.

"Those who are not of the wild life that we have chosen so bravely to live would have us remain under the boot heel of human servants and to be considered mere pets, objects of amusement noted for keeping the humans' blood pressure low."

Boos and hisses rang out from the crowd. Coal continued, and the crowd stopped to listen.

"Right you are, my army of wildcats. That is the image we are about to crush. The only thing standing in our way of total domination of the cat world and the world of humans is one cat and his rebellious army. Let the name "Dusty" ring foul in the mouth and mind of every wildcat. The battle we are about to fight will determine our victory or our defeat. And we shall be victorious!" shouted Coal. "Off now to your campsites. Sharpen your claws, and wet your warrior appetites. For tomorrow, victory shall be yours!"

The crowd again went wild with cheers and shouts as Coal slowly backed off the balcony into the relative silence of his room. He could hear the crowd as they shouted again and again, "Coal, Coal, Coal, Coal."

"Aah, listen to that, Major. This sound is music to my ears."

At that time, the beautiful black Maine Coon called Fortune walked into the room, pushing a stroller containing three sleeping Maine Coon-like kittens.

"Aah, Fortune, my dear. What a delightful surprise!" said Coal. "Oh, there are my three future conquerors sound asleep. Wonderful of you to bring them, my love.

However, you are quite late, my dear. The speech is over, and my army is reveling in the aftermath."

"Forgive me, my king." said Fortune. "The children were engaged in playing when I realized."

Coal held his paw up to stop her explanation.

"Think nothing of it, my dear. Mistakes happen."

Walking over to her, he ejected one of his claws and gently caressed Fortune from ear to ear with it.

"But I do hope in the future I can count on you being punctual? Especially when my children are involved."

"Y-yes. Of course, my king," said Fortune, her voice cracking in fear.

"Good!" shouted Coal.

One of the kittens stirred at Coal's loud voice.

"Oh, I mean good," said Coal, taking his voice down to a whisper. "Now, my dear, run along and settle the children in for the night. Tomorrow will be one of the biggest days of their life."

"As you wish, my lord," replied Fortune as she pushed the stroller out of the room and down the corridor.

Once Coal was sure Fortune was out of ear range, he turned to his ruthless assistant.

"Once the children have been settled for the night, I want you to eliminate Fortune," said Coal.

"You mean kill her, sir?" asked Thorn.

"Of course not, Major. I mean take her to a salon and give her a pedicure. Of course kill her, you flat pile of catnip!"

"Yes, sir!" shouted Thorn in fear. He then saluted and dismissed himself.

Coal drifted over to his bedroom throne and collapsed into its soft cushions as he propped his feet on the stool. His cat servants then came to his side. One began to massage his feet, and yet another rubbed his head.

"All the rewards of command," said Coal as he indulged in the attention he was receiving.

IN THE FOREST
OF MISSISSIPPI

"Quiet, quiet," said the black shorthair cat. "Allow General Fang to continue."

Fang, a very large albino mountain lion stepped forward to continue his briefing on the masters' battle plans. All of the felines were gathered around a model of Coal's mountain and the El Paso desert where the battle would be fought. Fang began, "I know many of you do not agree on the killing of an enemy, even if they are most particularly bent on killing you. However, that is why we hold the rank of cat masters. We have the fighting knowledge to take life or preserve it."

"Then let our lawyers make the judgment, General," said a margay in the crowd.

"This is a military matter, Colonel," said Fang, addressing the margay. Seven then stepped in to resolve the conflict.

"Quiet, everyone. Master Eight, our top keeper of the master law, will settle this issue so we can continue."

Out of the crowd stepped a very large blue British Shorthair wearing a monocle. Taking the monocle from his eye, he cleared his throat and began, "I say, Chaps, the law appears to be quite clear on this one point, I say, I say. The law of the masters, section one clearly states, 'If one possesses the knowledge to preserve life, then life must be preserved.' The only exception to this law would be section two that says, 'If two Masters are fighting each other, then the penalty for the violating Master would be death.' Since we are not at war with cats from the master clan, we are bound to preserve life at all cost."

The crowd went wild again with discussion.

Seven stepped forward.

"Quiet! That is it, and the matter is settled. We disable our enemy, but we do not kill them. Violators of the law will be punished. General Fang, please continue."

"Thank you, Master Seven. We have already received word from the king of this realm, King Sancho, that his forces will contain the area around the battlefield for several miles. No one gets in, and no one gets out. His brother, Alfanso, has also alerted many of his subjects living in Sancho's realm to aid Sancho's army in every way. Alfanso's air force will also aid us at the proper time. Since no one can get in or out, then we need not worry about elaborate flanking movements. It appears our strike will be a traditional frontal assault. According to the wildcat records of training, Coal was trained in the traditional cat schools. In other words, he is an academician and not a soldier. So we can safely deduce his thinking as far as warfare is concerned would be very two-dimensional. Most of the history Coal has read has been classical and very little, if any, of it has to do with tactics.

"We shall make a very impressive and forceful frontal assault against our enemy. If, in the unlikely event we are going to be outflanked, then our air force will take care of the problem. In light of the interpretation of the cat master's law we have just heard, I recommend we use the technique of *back paw* to stun and render our enemy helpless. As all of you know, this particular blow—when applied to the back of the head properly—will render the cat on the receiving end with an enormous headache and a lapse of memory of about one year. This should give us plenty of time to get the cats out of the area and give them a memory that has nothing to do with Coal or the war."

The crowd erupted with shouts and discussion of approval. Dusty leaned over and asked Seven, "What is the technique of *back paw?*"

"It is a strike behind the left ear, about here," said Seven as he pointed to his own head. "A strike here with enough force will render the opponent unconscious for a couple of hours. And the victim loses at least one year of memory."

"When do I learn that move?" asked Dusty.

"When you have studied enough to become a full cat master," replied Seven. "This particular blow in the hands of someone untrained can cause instant death."

"Now, everyone," shouted General Fang. "Move out. Get to the desert of El Paso by any means necessary. We have about twenty-four hours to pull this one off."

Suddenly, the relative quiet of the forest was disturbed by the flapping of wings. Red-tailed hawks, hundreds of them, landed on the forest floor. Sergeant Sky stepped forward and reported to Seven as the rest of the astonished cat masters gathered around.

"The royal air force of King Alfanso reporting for the service of the cat masters."

"Wonderful!" shouted General Fang. "Masters, begin sling load operations at once."

All the cat masters—working at a fevered pitch—fashioned straps from the vines in the forest. They split up into groups of four, strapping themselves together and then giving the remaining straps to four or five hawks as they held them in their talons. Then, like a single great bird, the group of hawks began flapping their wings and lifting the small group of cats high in the air and over the tops of the forest trees toward the desert of El Paso. This ritual was repeated again and again as hundreds of cat masters and red-tailed hawks took to the skies.

"When do we leave, master?" asked Dusty.

"Our ride is about to arrive," said Seven.

Looking upward, Dusty saw the grand sight of two giant bald eagles descending, barely making a sound as they glided to a stop on the forest floor. The other cats and birds took no notice as they continued their task of sling-load operations.

"Eeeeeah!" cried one of the eagles.

"You are most welcome, Boaz," replied Seven. "Dusty! These are the two great eagles of King Alfanso's realm. They have lived for seventy years along the Savannah River on the South Carolina side. This is Boaz, and this is Jachin. They will be our ride to the desert of El Paso."

Suddenly, Dusty felt ill. Gripping his stomach, he fell to his knees. Seven noticed other Maine Coons in the group gripping their stomachs at the same moment but brushed the incident aside to continue working.

"Master, what is wrong with me?"

"The sensation you are feeling is common among Maine Coons. Your race of cats has a very close connection with others of the same race. It is said that one Maine Coon can alert another Maine Coon when they are in trouble, but we don't even know how this is done. It is just an unexplained gift."

"Why are the other Maine Coons here unaffected?" asked Dusty.

"They have been, but they have more experience than you, and they have learned to control the pain much better. You will also in time, but for now, we must go. A Maine Coon is obviously in trouble, and it is no one here in this group. More than likely, our Maine Coon in trouble awaits us in the plain of El Paso."

Seven picked Dusty up and placed him on the saddle already secured to Jachin. Then Seven jumped on the saddle secured on Boaz.

"Cat masters!" yelled Seven. "To victory for the cat and human races!" Shouts of approval rang out from the remaining cats already being lifted into the air by the remaining hawks. Then Dusty and Seven were lifted swiftly into the air on the backs of the great eagles toward the distant land of El Paso.

THE PLAIN OF EL PASO

Thorn stood silent as he peered out of Coal's balcony window, looking through a set of human binoculars. Below on the El Paso plain, Thorn could see the one thousand strong cat army taking their formations of twenty-five, fifty or one hundred cat companies. Coal came and stood beside him.

"Aaah, Major, don't they look magnificent?" said Coal as he stroked his whiskers.

"Yes, my lord. The battle shall be a swift and decisive victory for you," replied Thorn.

"Thorn, old cat, have you taken care of the matter of Fortune we spoke about earlier?"

No, my lord."

"And why not?" shouted Coal, grabbing Thorn by the throat.

"B...b...because, my lord, the rocks!"

Coal released his loyal officer out of curiosity or surprise.

"Rocks?" asked Coal.

Gasping for air as he massaged his neck, Thorn replied, "Why, yes, my lord. First of all, the bird we chose to fly this mission needs sunlight to fly due to his poor vision. He will leave at dawn. Then he wanted to find a place most particularly jagged and secluded to hide the body. He was then going to fly as high as possible and then release her. The fall alone at that altitude should be enough to, shall we say, do away with any evidence," said Thorn as he broke into an evil smile.

Coal thought for a moment, scratching his chin.

"Yes. The idea has merit. I don't know why I doubted you, Major. Tell you what, take care of Fortune and destroy our enemy, and I will make you commanding general of all the wild armies."

"But you already have a general, my lord," said Thorn in surprise.

"Oh, that was this morning. He failed to lose our chess game this morning, so I fired him, reduced him to private, and threw him into jail. Congratulations, Major. You are now my brevet general until the outcome of the battle is decided."

Coal wrapped his arm around the now-terrified major. "Aah, General, your ambition for advancement has finally come to fruition."

"Yes, thank you, my lord," said Thorn nervously. "You're too kind, my lord."

"Yes, I know," said Coal, glancing at himself in the mirror. "Dawn is approaching. Summon the great buzzard, and do away with Fortune at once."

"Yes, my lord, at once," said Thorn.

SKYWARD

Meanwhile, high in the skies, heading toward the plains of El Paso, the sky was filled with red-tailed hawks carrying the famous cat masters toward the inevitable battle to free cat and human kind. Dusty and Seven were the only two riding eagles outfitted with saddles. Dusty grabbed his stomach again. The sick feeling he experienced earlier had returned.

"Master!" shouted Dusty to Seven. "This unexplained sickness has returned but much more powerful."

Seven quickly looked around at the other Maine Coons in the group. He did not even see any of them react at all as before. Seven sensed this was something different. Perhaps Dusty, being of two races of cats, had inherited another ability yet undiscovered.

But there is no time to figure that out now, thought Seven. "You need to get to El Paso before the rest of us, Dusty," commanded Seven. "I sense if you delay, it may be too late. Jachin!" he shouted. "Make haste."

The great eagle Dusty rode upon bent his head forward and gained speed. Faster and faster he went, passing hawk after hawk and cat after cat. In moments, Dusty realized he had left all the others behind, and he and Jachin were the only ones piercing the night air.

DEATH SCARE

Fortune gasped as the giant buzzard wrapped his talons around her shoulders and under her arms. The night air was extremely windy and cool. Coal and Thorn emerged from the secret door on top of the mountain to view the spectacle.

"Why are you doing this, Coal?" shouted Fortune.

"Don't take it so hard, my dear. You have served your purpose," replied Coal, unmoved by Fortune's cracking voice.

"But my kittens? Where are they, and what are you going to do with them?"

"Not to worry, my dear," replied Coal. "They are my problem now, and I will teach them all they need to know."

Fortune began to cry. "You just used me. You said you loved me, and the entire time you just wanted my cubs, my precious cubs, to do your dirty work? What exactly do you intend to teach them, Coal? The path of dishonesty? That cheating your fellow cat is the way to get ahead? How to use female cats for your own amusement?"

"Silence!" shouted Coal, slapping Fortune across the face. "Yes to all of your questions, Fortune, and believe me, I will teach them much more than that. They will see that my way is the only way to true victory, and I will demonstrate that to the entire cat race tonight. Oh, and one other lesson, my dear. Never hold on to dead weight in your business."

Thorn gave the signal to the great buzzard. Higher and higher the ugly bird rose into the air. Coal and Thorn became smaller and smaller to Fortune as she was taken ever higher into the sky. She could see the first hint of sunlight starting to illuminate the cloudy night sky. Then she saw it—a mass of rocky mountains banded together. The ugly bird sped toward the great mass of rocks until he was directly over it. He then picked up speed, flying straight up. Higher and higher he rose. The mountain of rocks grew smaller and smaller and eventually became hidden by the morning clouds over the desert. She began to have trouble breathing. Then, without warning, the ugly buzzard let Fortune go. Fortune began to regain her senses the closer to the ground she came. Piercing through the clouds she could see the great mountain of rocks appear. Fortune screamed at the top of her lungs but knew it was no use. There was no one to hear her, no one to help her as she came closer to the rocks. Then she subconsciously began her own countdown before her young life would end. Four, three, two, one. *Swoop*!

"Gotcha!" came a voice from nowhere.

Fortune realized she was no longer falling. She was flying. Opening her eyes, she saw the face of an orange Maine Coon.

"Hi. My name is Dusty," came the voice in Maine Coon.

"Who are you? Why are you here?" asked Fortune.

"Once again, the name is Dusty," said Dusty, half laughing. "Secondly, I am here rescuing you because I felt your presence screaming for help!"

"Thank the Great Cat!" shouted Fortune as she hugged Dusty's neck and gave him a big kiss on the cheek. "But my children?" said Fortune in desperation.

"Leave your children to me," said Dusty. "We know the battle is a distraction. Do you know where Coal intends to take the kittens when the battle begins?"

"Yes, steer your bird behind his mountain, and I will show you," said Fortune. "There. Do you see it? In the desert there, about a mile from this mountain. A trap door in the trunk of that desert tree. No one but Coal and myself, and of course his toad Thorn know about it."

"Very well then, princess. We will be ready for him," said Dusty. "Jachin? Let us return to the main group."

The massive eagle turned slowly and headed back to the battlefront with great speed.

A BATTLE OF CATS

There on the plain of El Paso, the cat masters gathered in their formations, looking much like the Roman legions of old. General Fang stood, staring at the open plain with only Coal's mountain breaking the outline of the desert skyline. The sun was visible now as the entire desert became illuminated.

"What are the numbers, Sergeant?" asked Fang of Sky, the red-tailed hawk.

"My last fly-by indicated about three thousand wildcats to include the ferals, General."

"Very well," said Fang.

"Well, General, are you ready for the greatest of all the battles you have ever fought?" asked Seven.

"Ready as I am ever going to be, Master Seven."

At that moment, Jachin swooped into a landing. Dusty jumped off the large eagle's back and then helped Fortune step down.

"We have the location of Coal's escape with the children, Master Seven," reported Dusty.

"Very well," said Fang. "Master Seven, I recommend that you and Dusty outflank Coal and wait for him at the disclosed location. I will direct the main effort here. We may fail here, but you must not fail in intercepting the kittens. Everything depends on it."

"You can count on us, General," replied Seven. "Come, Dusty, let us be on our way."

"Please, Master Seven, don't let anything happen to my children. They cannot help who their father may be. I alone am at fault for that."

"Their father has nothing to do with who they will become, my dear. Rest assured we will do what is right by your children."

In a flash, Dusty and Master Seven once again mounted Jachin and Boaz—the great eagles—to fly to their location.

—◦◦◦—

Meanwhile, back at Coal's mountain, Coal stepped out on the balcony to observe all the cat formations below him. Looking through his human-made binoculars, Thorn could plainly see the cat masters' formations developing.

"They are ready to attack, my lord," said Thorn. "However, this does not seem to be the run-of-the-mill army. We may yet have a fight on our hands."

"Fear not, Major. We are more than a match for anything that boy can muster. Anyway, is the bassinet with the children ready?"

"It is, my lord," replied Thorn.

"Give the signal to attack."

Thorn picked up a conch shell and blew it, sounding the charge. A long mournful sound flowed from the shell. The signal to attack had been given. The massive formations below shouted with glee and began to move forward—first with a walk, then a trot, then a gallop, then the entire group was running at full cat speed.

—◦◦◦—

Meanwhile, on the cat masters' side of the field, Fang watched the oncoming cloud of dust with the calm of a skilled and experienced warrior. Turning to the massive formations of the cat masters, Fang spoke as a true general.

"My fellow warriors, I implore you to remember it is not about us. It never has been. It's about doing the harder right. Fighting for those who cannot fight for themselves. We are massively outnumbered. Our latest count reveals they have a ten-to-one ratio in their favor. So every cat here must take out ten cats in order to bring total victory. In the words of the great cat, 'Greater love hath no cat than to lay down his life for another cat.' And in this case, that includes our humans. Cat masters, move out!"

The cat masters began to move forward. They moved as one group, barely kicking up dust or making a sound. When they reached their running speed, it looked as if they glided on air.

Closer and closer the two massive armies raced toward each other. Closer and closer they came. At the right moment, Fang let out an incredible yet familiar scream of the mountain lions. Then the outer formations of the cat masters began to spread out to gradually encircle the approaching force. Then with all the speed the two armies could muster, they collided. The sound of flesh striking flesh and the variety of screams from cats deafened the sounds of the desert floor as a cloud of dust engulfed the two armies.

—⁓—

Up in Coal's quarters overlooking the battleground, Thorn continued to look through the human binoculars. Coal had grabbed the handle of the carriage containing the kittens when he saw Thorn looking intently at what was happening on the battlefield.

"Thorn, what in the world are you looking at?"

"Sir, the battle is obscured from view because of the dust. I can't tell who's winning," said Thorn with alarm in his voice.

"No one is a match for my army!" shouted Coal. "Now get over here and help me get these kittens out of here."

"Yes, my lord," replied Thorn as he put down his binoculars and grabbed a book on the nearby bookshelf.

Thorn pulled the book forward, and the walls behind the canopy bed separated, revealing a secret passage.

"Quickly!" shouted Coal as both he and Thorn with the carriage of kittens disappeared through the secret passage.

—◦◦◦—

Outside on the battlefield, the sound of fighting continued. Wildcats would lunge for their target, sometime eight or nine of them to one cat master, only to be knocked unconscious by the cat master in a matter of seconds. Wildcat after wildcat hit the ground unaware that they were even in the world. Other wildcats began to notice as the battle went on that they were completely surrounded.

"It's a trap!" shouted one of the wildcats, only to feel the painful blow to the back of his head.

—◦◦◦—

Suddenly, the darkness of the secret passage lit up as the double doors opened in the massive desert tree trunk. Thorn and the carriage of three precious wild and Maine Coon-mixed kittens walk out into a clearing in the desert. Coal and Thorn walk out with the carriage when the kittens begin to cry.

"Oh! What now?" shouted Coal. "Here we are in the middle of an escape, and they start crying."

"I think they are hungry," came a voice from among the desert foliage.

"Who said that?" asked Coal.

Dusty and Master Seven appeared from behind a desert yucca plant.

"Why, I did," replied Seven. "Now if you don't mind, I will take those children off of your paws, and you can go back to the El Paso zoo for the rest of your life."

Seven picked up a smooth, long staff from behind the yucca plant.

"Ha!" shouted Coal. "No weasel domestic cat taunts me. Thorn, guard the children while I take care of this bothersome old domestic."

"Dusty!" said Seven.

"Yes, Master. I am on the kittens."

Then, without warning, Coal lunged for both Dusty and Seven with lightning speed. Seven pushed Dusty out of the way and slapped Coal beside the face with the staff, sending him to the ground with a thud! Dusty quickly gathered his thoughts, got up, and made his way to the carriage. Thorn braced for the attack and leapt for Dusty. Instinctively, Dusty skillfully moved to one side, struck Thorn in his stomach with a back kick and then sent him flying face-long into the tree trunk with one strike to Thorn's back. Thorn flattened out against the tree and slid down to the ground unconscious. Dusty, still standing in his combat pose, was stunned at what just happened.

Did I do that? thought Dusty. He quickly shook off the effects of his own shocking defense and grabbed the carriage.

Dusty opened the carriage cover to reveal the half-wild, half-Maine Coon kittens smiling at him like a long-lost friend.

———✦———

Meanwhile, Coal continued to lunge at Seven. Each time, Seven struck Coal in a different area of his anatomy. *Foop! Pow! Slap!* Finally Coal raised himself from the desert floor as blood dripped from his mouth and ears.

"This cannot be," said Coal. "There is no way that a mere domestic breed cat can defeat the likes of a panther that outweighs him by one hundred pounds. This simply cannot be, you hear?"

Coal lunged once again in a desperate attempt to make his worst nightmare go away. *Throt!* Dusty looked and saw Coal pinned to the ground, stiff as a board as Master Seven stood on his chest with his staff wedged in Coal's neck.

"Oh, it simply can be, my dear Coal," replied Master Seven. "You will observe that you cannot move your head or control your own facial muscles. Do you know why? There is a simple nerve that runs along this side of your head, and my staff is pressing on it right now. For all of your physical might, Coal, you are now controlled by a simple nerve on the side of your skull. Very humbling, isn't it?"

"You will pay for this!" mumbles Coal.

"I don't think so, Coal, because in one second, you will not even remember this event happened."

Seven quickly removed the staff from Coal's head and struck him behind the ear.

THE AFTERMATH

Finally, the dust cleared as the final wildcat fell to the desert floor unconscious. Fang walked through the aftermath, observing the results of the battle.

A Russian Blue walked up to Fang and reported, "General, all of the wildcats have been rendered disabled."

"Very good, Captain," replied Fang.

"Your orders, sir?" replied the Russian blue.

"Take Coal's mountain fortress, and shut it down. Leave no trace of his activities for our human counterparts to find. The secret of our special powers must be kept from the humans. Next, have the hawks fly another sling-load operation, and have all of the wildcats taken to various locations. They must not see each other when they awaken, or they may have total recall of their treacherous deeds."

"And what about Master Seven and his apprentice, Dusty, General?"

"I have a feeling they are taking care of things on their end. The less we know, the better."

COLUMBIA

In the halls of the Riverbanks Zoo, Alfanso is waiting patiently in his ready room before addressing the cat council. *For sure we would have word before the next meeting of the council on the progress of our man, Dusty,* thought Alfanso. Suddenly, a very out-of-breath Captain Domingo ran into the room.

"My lord!" shouted Domingo.

Outside, the council gathered at night, waiting patiently at the auditorium of the old bridge ruins between the zoo and the botanical gardens. Without warning, Alfanso walked on stage under the spotlight. The crowd immediately quieted down.

"My fellow felines," began Alfanso. "Dusty has been victorious! Coal and his entire army have been defeated!"

Shouts and cheers followed by meows of joy rang out from the crowd. Priscilla once again fainted in the arms of Saja, her butler. As the elation of the crowd continued, Domingo leaned over to speak in Alfanso's ear.

"What of the kittens, my lord?"

"I was assured by the head cat master himself that our cat, Dusty, took care of the problem with bravery and dispatch," replied Alfanso. "By the way, Captain, draw up a proclamation for the council to sign. As requested by Dusty, the domestic half-breed cats will be recognized as a pride with full representation in the Cat Council of the Carolina realm. Dusty will be granted a seat on the council as their representative. See to it he is at the next meeting. I should like to recognize our new hero."

"It shall be done, my lord."

—◦⁄◦◦—

Three months later.

Dusty sat on the balcony railing of the second floor of the apartment where his human servants lived. There was a beautiful cool morning breeze flowing through Three Rivers apartment complex, and the shade cast by the pine trees made the evening most agreeable.

"You look very relaxed," came a voice from the sliding glass door.

Out on the balcony walked Lydia. Dusty jumped down and gave her a lick on the side of her face.

"Lydia, my love, how did you sneak past mom and dad servant?"

"Oh, I have my ways, Dusty. Besides a girl has to keep coming around a fellow to show she is interested in him until he is willing to give her a proposal of some sort."

Dusty clung at his throat a little.

"Why, yes, my dear. I see what you mean."

"Don't have a heart attack, Dusty. I can wait until you're ready. On another subject, my reluctant soul mate, do you think the kittens will be all right?"

"As long as their existence remains a secret. If either the wildcats or the kingdoms of the lions find out, they could be in jeopardy. Every time Master Seven comes to Columbia to continue my training, he gives me a report on the kittens and their mother, Fortune. They are all very happy living in the Mississippi forest with Master Seven."

"What about Fortune? Will there be any charges brought against her for consenting to Coal's marriage and having his children?" asked Lydia.

"According to Alfanso's royal lawyer, it would not be prudent to bring charges against a now-single mother and one that has apparently lost her kittens. So they have sent her into exile in the custody of the now known cat masters."

"Dusty, will the revealing of the cat masters be a problem for them to continue their work?"

"Not really. No one has officially seen a cat master in this realm. Though their existence has many believers, there is no one that can actually prove their existence.

There is already a rumor that *Cat Master* was actually a code name for Sancho's forces."

"I wonder who started spreading that rumor," said Lydia, looking at Dusty. Dusty gave a shy smile. "But will the children turn out all right? I mean, will they be moral?" asked Lydia. "After all, they did have such an evil father."

"I have learned a whole lot about all of this," replied Dusty. "It is not about who your earthly parents are. It is about who you're going to follow and obey in life. All we can do, my love, is teach the kittens the right way. What is it the Great One was quoted as saying? 'Raise a cat up in the way that he should go, and when he is old, he will not depart from it.' The kittens will one day come to a point in their lives that they will simply have to make a choice—to follow evil or to follow good. The same choice we all have had to make."

"Now who taught you that?" asked Lydia, smiling at Dusty.

"An old cat master of the Great One," replied Dusty with a smile.